Kite Flying in the Village

A Guyanese Girl's Story

Myrtle Watson

AuthorHouse™
1663 Liberty Drive
Bloomington, IN 47403
www.authorhouse.com
Phone: 1-800-839-8640

First published by AuthorHouse   02/11/2011

ISBN: 978-1-4520-8632-3 (sc)

Library of Congress Control Number: 2010915480

Printed in the United States of America

Certain stock imagery © Thinkstock.

This book is printed on acid-free paper.

authorHOUSE®

Acknowledgments

This story is written for my oldest grandchildren, Malcolm, Jasmine, Audrey and Raeven. You have given me the greatest gift. Reading my childhood stories to you is most delightful. Your simple words of encouragement mean more to me than you will ever know. I still remember the statement, "Granny, your stories are very good and other children would love to read them too". Thanks to all of you, I am enjoying my new career.

Kite Flying in the Village

My name is Anya, and I am nine years old. I live with my mother, father, sister and three brothers in a small village, Vreedenhoop, in Guyana, South America.

Easter is a very special holiday in our village. After church on Easter Sunday morning, my three brothers, sister, and I eat our lunches as fast as a hare, for we have much to do. Today is the day we will make our kites, and we are very excited.

We rush from the dinner table and down the stairs. Outside, we see Dad cutting the frames for our kites from the stems of coconut branches. We scurry around him. I see the boy next door. His name is Joey. He is peeking through the fence. He does not know I am watching him. I see him struggling, trying to cut his own frame without any help from a parent.

My family takes turns cutting colorful thin paper into squares and triangles. We make paste for our kites with flour and water. We also use a wild berry, known as Gamma Cherry. It is a very sticky fruit.

My brothers make box -shaped kites. My sister and I make triangle- shaped ones. We make our kites with bright, illuminating colors, and various shapes and sizes. We decorate our kites with frills made of very thin shreds of paper. My brothers stick eyes, ears, noses and mouths on their kites. The faces they design are scary, and we tell them so.

Daddy adds the tails to our kites. He makes them from strips of cloth, like old bed sheets. Each thin strip is about five feet long and an inch wide. We then tie our kites' tails with eight small bows about every six to eight inches apart from the beginning to the end of the tail. These bows give our kites a colorful rainbow tail. "I cannot wait for tomorrow to fly my kite," I say to my dad.

I awake before dawn, but everyone else is still asleep. I am so happy. I lay quietly waiting. It is Easter Monday, the morning after Easter Sunday, and another day of celebration and lots of fun for my family.

The brilliant sunrays shine through my bedroom windowpanes. I jump out of bed like a jackrabbit. I shout to my sister who is fast asleep. "Get up Pat! It is Easter Monday! We are going to fly our kites today!"

We dress in a hurry and rush off to the kitchen. We run, jostling each other along the way. We eat our breakfast as fast as we can and scamper off to get our kites. We set out with our mom and dad to go to the sea wall to meet our friends from the village. We hop and skip along the journey, chatting with each other. We hold our kites very tightly over our backs as we walk along the red, dusty road and through the howling wind. I look back over my shoulder. A few feet away Joey is trailing alone behind us.

We arrive at the sea wall and Mom picks a picnic spot. Daddy takes us to the open and sandy area. The sea wall is a long concrete walkway jutting out into the Atlantic Ocean. This concrete walkway is also called a "Jetty". It is a breakwater that prevents the ocean from flowing inland when the tide rises high.

When we are ready, Dad holds our kites one by one. Each of us holds the twine or string from our kite. We walk forward about twenty feet. Our hands are above our heads, and then we all burst full speed ahead like wild dogs chasing after rabbits.

Each kite lifts higher and higher into the air as it sways to the gentle breeze. The kites soar up to the clear blue sky as the wind blows stronger and longer. We unravel the twine from the stick by twisting our wrists to make a figure eight. This motion allows our kites to dance up and away across the pale blue sky.

I hold my kite as tightly as I can. Suddenly, on the tip of my toes, I feel my feet lifting off from the ground to soar with my kite. As I stare into the clear blue sky, I whisper to Pat, "Look!"

I see a million kites dancing above my head. Their tails swing back and forth, sometimes locking with each other, tangling as they plummet from the sky to the ground.

Pat and I hang on to our kites with both hands. We hope our kites will not be lost forever. The music of the kites is fun for all the boys and girls. It is a high-pitched noise, "Hue-eu-eu-eu and buzz buzzing!" that sounds like a million bees to me. Others even roar like baby lions. Can you imagine several kites making these sounds all together? It is awesome. Pat and I love to listen to the music of the kites.

One after another, kites break away and sail higher and farther. I can only see specks that disappear behind fluffy white pillows of low clouds. I stand helpless as a little girl runs to her dad crying, "My kite is gone!"

Joey is here too. No one wants to play with him. He laughs at the little girl like some of the other boys. He has tied a flat razor blade at the end of his kite's tail. He is very good at making his kite do circular loops. This allows him to cut the twine of another child's kite.

A kite war of sorts sends chills up my spine as I watch my kite string cut. It flies away and simply disappears. Off I run screaming "Daddy! Daddy!" still holding on to the string of my kite. "What will I fly now?" I ask. He gently whispers in my ear, "Pat will share her kite with you."

We are at the sea wall all day long. Families dress in tropical colors of bright red, canary-yellow, green and orange. Broad rim hats cover some of their faces from the brilliant sun. Steel band music plays in the background and adds to the festivities of a grand picnic.

People sit around the sandy shores for many hours. Dads tell stories to the children. Moms churn and serve homemade ice cream. My friends and I play hopscotch and marbles in the sand when we take a break from flying our kites. During the break, we tie our kites to rocks and leave them to the control of the winds.

I am lucky I have a caring father to help me and my sister and my brothers make our kites and a loving mother to go with us for a picnic too. I notice Joey standing all alone at the Easter Monday kite festival. I walk over to him and say, "Joey why did you cut down my kite?" Joey's face is red. He looks away and bows his head. He is sorry for what he has done. I place my hand over his shoulder and say, "Joey come on over with my family for some ice-cream. Would you like that?" Joey looks up at me with a broad smile. Together we join the family festivities. I shout, "Hey everyone this is Joey!"

They are all surprised to see Joey. Everyone knows that none of the children in the village play with Joey. He is always in trouble at school. My dad walks over. He reaches out his long, strong arms and circles Joey in a great big hug.

The day ends as the sun begins to set in the west. The sun casts a deep orange halo below the horizon. We pull our kites down one by one from the dusky, grey sky. We wind the twine back on the stick, place our kites over our shoulders and off we go to our homes. Some of our kites are tattered and torn. I whisper to Pat, "Tomorrow we can fly kites again," and she replies, "Yay! No school!"

Pat, my brothers and I cannot wait for tomorrow. All of our friends in the village will come to our house in the morning. We invite Joey to come too. We will fly our kites in the neighborhood streets.

My new kite soars up above my head and into a nearby tree it clings. I tug the string as hard as I can. It breaks from my kite. Joey scampers over to the tree. He climbs higher and higher. He reaches for my kite and looks at me. I realize Joey wants to have friends too. All the children shout "Hooray" for Joey.

He climbs down the tree, clutching my kite to his chest. I say to Pat, "Do you think Joey remembers the kindness we showed him yesterday?" Pat says, "One good turn deserves another!" "Clip-clop" she skips away down the street and runs to the house. At the end of another day, some of our kites are lost, but Joey now has many new friends in the village. Kite flying is fun for friends and for families.

Myrtle Watson was born in Guyana, South America. Her husband is Edmund S. Watson. They have four children. Their boys are Stephen, Sean, and Scott and their daughter, Sharon. The Watsons have nine grand children. Their ages range from one to eighteen. Myrtle's husband moved to Washington D.C. to attend college in 1968 and she joined him one year later. In 1975 they moved to Tulsa, OK, where they still reside.

As a mother of four young children, she worked as a part-time nurse on the labor and delivery unit at Saint Francis Hospital. This became the biggest juggling act of her life, keeping up with home and their children was an enormous challenge but she would do it again if she had to, without hesitation. Myrtle is presently working for The Margaret Hudson Program, a non-profit organization. The Margaret Hudson Program is for school-aged girls that are either pregnant and/or parenting teens. Myrtle enjoys her family's many traditions which include dancing to West Indies music, laughing, and loving.

Myrtle's hobbies are cooking, writing, reading, gardening and putting together Watson family albums. She likes to think of it as telling her family's story from past to present. Myrtle's goal is to become a children's author, the only career change of her life. Her desire is to write for children between the ages of preschool to preteens. She started writing ten years ago for her grandchildren. They told her that other children would love her stories. Myrtle thought this was a great compliment.

Myrtle's ultimate goal is to write several stories from her childhood; in these stories she would like to inform children of her cultural childhood and broaden the reader's knowledge of diversity at a young age.

CPSIA information can be obtained at www.ICGtesting.com
224334LV00003B